Sea Monsters
Coloring Book

Peter F. Copeland

D1408298

DOVER PUBLICATIONS
Garden City, New York

INTRODUCTION

A monster is generally regarded as too strange, too frightening, or too huge to be real or to engender belief. Yet throughout history, people everywhere have been fascinated by tales of these nightmarish creatures, so many of which exist—or are thought to exist—in the unexplored depths of the ocean. Philosophers and artists of ancient times described and illustrated these behemoths of the deep, and later discoveries taught us that at least some of these creatures—the giant squid among them—do in fact exist.

Sightings of gigantic sea serpents and huge marine lizards have been reported for as long as mankind has been keeping such records, but no one knows for sure whether they ever actually existed. As recently as 1983, a California construction crew claimed to have seen a huge serpent basking in the waters of the Pacific, just off the coast of Marin County. But without collaborative evidence such as photographs, it is difficult to conclusively prove its existence or uncover its true identity.

Some of the monsters shown in this book, such as the Ocean Dragon and the Great Bardfysshe, are obviously fables, beasts of legend that never were. Others like the Komodo lizard and the double-crested crocodile, we now know are indeed real, living breathing creatures of our own time. Then there are those whose existence is questionable, like the giant octopus of St. Malo and the various serpents sighted off the Atlantic coast in the last century. They may be living fossils, or creatures which have so far eluded scientific detection, and may still survive somewhere in the ocean's depths today.

The next time you are at the beach, look out over the vast expanse of water and think of the yet unknown and unimagined creatures that may live in its depths. Look over there, where an indistinct shape is breaking the surface, out near the horizon—is it a dolphin, a porpoise, or . . . something else?

Dedication

For Colton Thomas

Bibliographical Note

Sea Monsters Coloring Book is a new work, first published by Dover Publications in 1999.

International Standard Book Number

ISBN-13: 978-0-486-40562-9
ISBN-10: 0-486-40562-1

Manufactured in the United States of America
40562112   2022
www.doverpublications.com

THE GREAT NORWAY KRAKEN

The ancient peoples of Scandinavia believed that the Kraken—a horned sea monster—was the largest creature in the world, so large in fact that it was sometimes mistaken for a group of islands by sailors far from shore. In the 18th century, Erik Ludvigsen Pontoppidan, a Scandinavian bishop, claimed the Kraken could grasp and sink even the biggest ships. Pictured above is this huge lizard seizing and destroying a medieval trading vessel called a "cog." The Kraken of yore is now believed by some scientists to have been the forebear of the giant squid.

THE TUSKED PIG WHALE OF MOZAMBIQUE

Portuguese explorers of the late 15th century reported encountering a whale-like creature with huge boar-like tusks off the coast of Mozambique in southeast Africa. It was much like several similar sea monsters described and illustrated by cosmographer, Sebastian Münster, in his *Cosmographia* (Basel, 1550). The creature was said to be curious about the object floating next to it, but did the explorers no actual harm; it merely deluged them with clouds of spray and steam erupting from the the twin spouts in its head.

THE STRONSA BEAST OF 1808

In 1808, the Reverend Donald Maclean reported an encounter with a huge serpent-like creature while boating off the isle of Coll in the Orkneys. He described the animal as seventy to eighty feet long with a broad head and long neck. As it approached, Maclean and the other occupants beached their boat before fleeing for the shore. A number of fishermen on the nearby isle of Canna reported seeing the monster soon afterward. And later still, the body of a "huge animal of strange appearance" was washed up on the Orkney island of Stronsa. It was described as having a long neck and several pairs of fins, and a winding tail like that of a lizard.

Edward Home, a Scottish surgeon and naturalist, later identified the beast as a basking shark. But its true identity—sea serpent or shark?—remained a matter of heated controversy for some time.

3

THE GIANT PHYSETER OF 1455

In *Naturalist History,* Pliny the Elder's great compendium of the ancient sciences, he describes the Physeter as the "Blower," which "stands up like a huge column, higher than a ship's masts and spouts a torrent of water." Above we see an enraged Physeter confronting a Turkish Lateen rigged merchantman of the 15th century. This creature too—like the Norway Kraken—is believed by some to be an early appearance of the giant squid.

A FEARFUL ENCOUNTER WITH A GIANT OCTOPUS
IN THE BONIN ISLANDS, JAPAN, 1835

Thomas Beal, the surgeon of a British whaling vessel, described being attacked by a very large octopus while walking on a deserted island off southern Japan in 1835. Another victim of an octopus attack, a seafarer named Arthur Grimble, described his experience as follows: "I remember chiefly a dreadful [creature] with a Herculean power behind it . . . I could have sworn the brute's eyes burned at me . . . something whipped round my left arm and the back of my neck . . . I felt it crawling down the back of my shirt . . . a mouth began to nuzzle below my throat . . . the suckers felt like hot rings pulling at my skin." In both of these attacks, the victims were fortunate enough to be rescued from a horrible fate by their companions.

THE SEA DEVIL OF THE ADRIATIC, 1421

A huge serpent was said to have attacked a Venetian merchantman in the Adriatic Sea in 1421. The creature was described as having a long snake-like tongue and claws that resembled the talons of an eagle. Such reports as this one caused many early European seafarers to believe that the Sea of Darkness (the Atlantic Ocean) teemed with such monsters, providing them with a reason why so many sailors who ventured out upon its stormy waters never returned.

AN OCEAN DRAGON OF 1500

The medieval naturalist and physician Conrad von Gesner, in his *Historia animalium* of 1551, described a frightening creature more than 300 feet long, called an "Ocean Dragon." It was said to attack ships and sailors with claws and fangs.

Curiously, the ancient Chinese also described a great "Lung Wang"—or "Dragon King"—who lived in the sea. They believed it to be the first stage of the animal's existence in its evolution from a water snake to a winged dragon.

THE KOMODO DRAGON OF INDONESIA

Pictured above is a modern sea monster—the Komodo dragon—which inhabits Komodo Island in Indonesia. Although this creature has a 100 million year history, it has only been known outside of its native home since 1912. It is actually a giant monitor lizard that can grow to a length of more than ten feet, generally reaches a weight of 300 pounds, and may live 100 years. It is known to attack and devour the fishermen and boatmen who frequent the waterways around Komodo and the adjacent islands. In addition to this fearsome beast, there are more scorpions, spiders, poisonous snakes, and man-eating sharks in and around these islands than anywhere else in the world.

THE MANED SEA SERPENT OF BERGEN, NORWAY, 1755

Olaus Magnus, a Swedish cleric and historian of the mid-16th century, first described the "Sjö Orm" (Sea Snake): "[a] Sea Serpent of a length of upwards of 200 feet and 20 feet in diameter [which] lives in rocks and holes near the shore of Bergen. It comes out of its cavern only in summer nights and in fine weather to destroy calves, lambs or hogs, and goes into the water to eat Cuttles, Lobster, and all kinds of sea crabs . . . It has brilliant flaming eyes." The above depicts a later sighting of the creature—in 1755—with the serpent being fired upon by a party of boatmen on the Bergen fjord.

THE GREAT ICELANDIC SEA SNAKE OF 1568

Old Icelandic chronicles tell of sea monsters that are believed to inhabit the waters surrounding the island. In 1568, one such sea snake—as pictured above—is reported to have attacked and sank a fishing vessel near Skalholt, and devoured a luckless fisherman. Nurturing belief in this early sighting are the words of Eggert Ólafsson, the pioneering 18th-century naturalist, who wrote that "there is found in the Gulf of Hornefjord a quantity of eels, the length and thickness of which terrify the inhabitants of this country."

THE GREAT BARDFYSSHE OF 1571

In his *Cosmographia*, Sebastian Münster describes the bardfysshe as "an enormous creature with terrible tusks and horrifying horns and eyes, sixteen to twenty feet across . . ." Above we see a bardfysshe confronting a Portuguese galleon in 1571.

MALAY RAFTSMEN ATTACKED BY GIANT DOUBLE-CRESTED CROCODILES

The double-crested crocodile can grow to more than twenty feet in length and is found in the coastal waters of the Malay archipelago, northern Australia, and sometimes as far away as the Fiji Islands in the south Pacific Ocean. Above, a group of Malay raftsmen are attacked by two of these man-eating monsters.

SEA SERPENT SEEN OFF THE MASSACHUSETTS COAST IN 1817

The sea serpent was no stranger to American waters. There are tales of gigantic water serpents among the legends of many Native American tribes. The first sighting in the New World occurred in 1639, when a huge snake was seen laying coiled upon a rock in the harbor of Cape Ann, Massachusetts. In August of 1817, the *Salem Gazette* published an account of repeated sightings of a sea serpent seen "playing about" Gloucester Harbor, off Cape Anne, not far from the 1639 site: Hundreds of "respectable citizens" saw "a prodigious snake . . . from 50 to 100 feet [in length] . . . [H]is motions are serpentine, extremely varied, and exceedingly rapid." Above we see the creature approaching an early steam vessel off the coast of Massachusetts.

THE SCHOONER *SALLY* ENCOUNTERS A MONSTER SERPENT, 1819

From the early 18th century onward, there were many reports of encounters with sea serpents along the American east coast. Depicted above is one rather famous instance that allegedly occurred just off the coast of Long Island in December, 1819. The American schooner *Sally* was menaced by a fearsome serpent with a "dreadful head."

SEA SERPENT DESTROYING A FISHING BOAT
OFF THE COAST OF MASSACHUSETTS, 1819

The years between 1817 and 1847 represented the high point of sea monster activity off the Atlantic coast, all the way from Nova Scotia to South Carolina. Sightings of sea serpents became commonplace. The destruction of a fishing boat by a giant serpent was recorded in a painting of that time, on which the above illustration is based.

LONG-NECKED SERPENT SIGHTED OFF THE COAST OF BRAZIL, 1905

In 1905, two naturalists—fellows of the London Zoological Society—while aboard the steam yacht *Valhalla*, sighted a monster with a huge turtle-like head, a long neck as thick as "a slight man's body," and a six-foot long "fin or frill" protruding from the water: "it moved its head from side to side in a peculiar manner, the color of the head and neck was dark brown above and whitish below . . ." The illustration above derives from a drawing of the creature made for the London Zoological Society by one of the scientists who spotted the animal.

GIANT SQUID ATTACKING A FISHING DORY OFF ST. JOHN'S, NEWFOUNDLAND, 1873

One morning in the year 1873, two fishermen and a boy were rowing out into Conception Bay to net herring when they were attacked by a giant squid floating on the surface of the sea. Within a few seconds, the behemoth had enclosed the boat in its tentacles and was dragging it toward its open mouth. The boat began flooding as the tentacles were pulling it under. While one man rowed desperately toward the shore, the other began bailing out the boat—and the boy hacked at one of the huge tentacles with a hatchet. Fortunately, he was able to sever the tentacle coiling over the dory, at which point the monster retreated, emitting clouds of inky black fluid upon the water. The portion of the severed tentacle left clinging to the boat was nineteen feet long. The length of an ordinary giant squid is said to be about 50 feet (including tentacles). Whale carcasses found with eighteen-inch sucker scars point to the existence of squid more than 120 feet in length. But since the scar grows as the whale grows, it alone does not provide conclusive evidence.

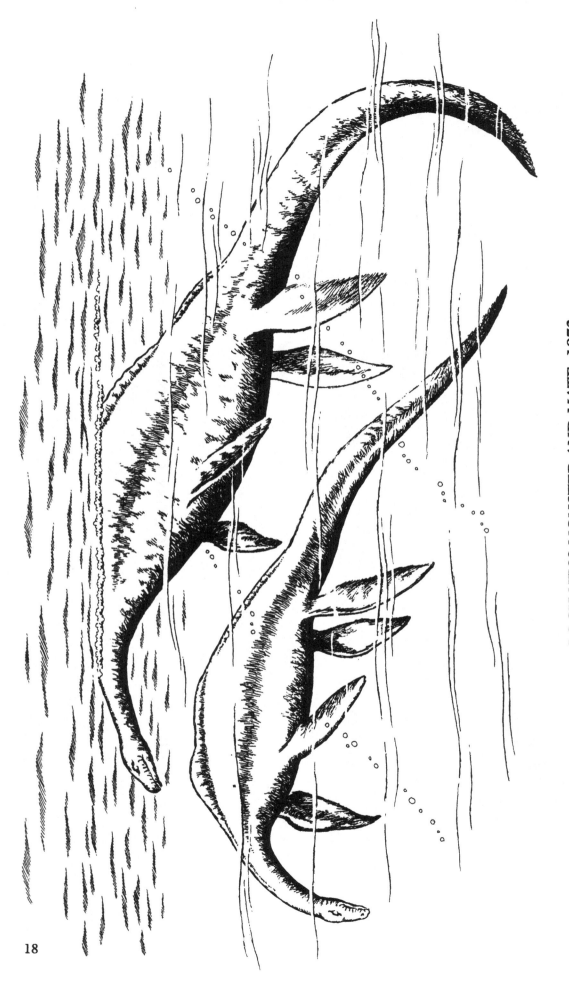

LOCH NESS MONSTER AND MATE, 1973

Loch Ness in the Scottish highlands is Europe's third largest body of fresh water, and probably its most mysterious. One of its most distinctive characteristics is its unusually great depth—in some spots it is more than 700 feet deep. Since 1880—the first modern-day eyewitness account of the monster's appearance—repeated sightings both genuine and fraudulent have been reported of a monster living in Loch Ness. Throughout history, accounts of such monsters living in inland lakes in—among other places—Norway, Iceland, and Sweden, as well as in native American fables and legends, have been recorded. Many believe that "Nessie" may be a surviving Plesiosaur from the Mesozoic era—about 225 million to 65 million years ago—when dinosaurs ruled the earth. Others think it may be a huge eel. This illustration of "Nessie" and mate is from a 1973 painting called "Courtship in Loch Ness."

OCTOPUS ATTACKING A SHIP OFF ANGOLA, 1802

In 1802, off the coast of Angola in southwest Africa, a creature described as a giant octopus was said to have attacked a French sailing ship, attempting to drag the ship down by winding its arms about the masts and sinking her. The terrified seamen made a vow to St. Thomas that—if delivered from this dreadful state—they would make a pilgrimage to his shrine. With cutlasses and axes the men were able to hack away at the monster's arms, causing him to loosen his hold and flee. When the ship reached St. Malo, the crew hastened to the chapel of St. Thomas, and commissioned a votive painting of their fearful encounter which survives to this day.

BATTLE BETWEEN A SPERM WHALE AND A GIANT SQUID

Such an encounter as the one depicted above has never been witnessed by man; but it is well known that giant squid engage in terrible battles with sperm whales, although most such battles take place under the sea and not on the surface as seen here. The enormous size of such a squid as the one pictured above may be deduced from the portions of squid tentacles found in the bellies of captured whales—one of which was found to be as thick as a stout man's body. Attached to it were several sucking disks as large as saucers, set around with claw-like hooks the size of tiger's teeth.

PERSEUS RESCUES ANDROMEDA FROM A FEROCIOUS DRAGON

Perseus, a hero of Greek mythology and a dragon-slayer of note, rescues the maid Andromeda, daughter of the King of Ethiopia, from a terrible sea dragon sent to ravage the country by the sea god Poseidon. Perseus succeeds in killing the monster and—according to legend—marries Andromeda.

THE STEAM TUG *CHURCHILL* ENCOUNTERS A GIANT SEA SNAKE, 1884

In August of 1884, the captain and deck watch of the steam tug *Churchill*, lying at anchor off Port Natal, South Africa, saw "a huge beast which suddenly appeared level with the bulwarks presenting a most terrific appearance,—it seemed covered with large sea shells and to have a big hairy head . . . its head could be seen some distance at one side [of the ship] while the tail was still visible many yards away at the other,—its length was estimated to be sixty feet."

THE AMBIZE OF THE CONGO

Also called the "Angulo" or "hogfish" by the people of the Congo, this is a fish monster believed to live on the shores of the Congo River in Africa. According to folk legends, it has the body of a fish, the muzzle and head of an ox, a pair of hands, and a tail shaped like a target. It is believed to live on a diet of river grass, and grows to a weight of more than 500 pounds. Natives of this region say that its flesh has the flavor of pork.

THE SERPENT OF THE *SACRAMENTO*

Captain W. H. Nelson of the American ship *Sacramento* reported that on her passage from New York to Melbourne, Australia, he and his men sighted a sea serpent in mid-Atlantic which they were able to thoroughly scrutinize. Forty feet of the creature was visible. The captain reported that it was as thick as a flour barrel, and yellowish-brown in color with the head of an alligator and a pair of flippers. Above we see the animal competing with the seabirds for fish.

SCUBA DIVER ATTACKED BY A GREAT WHITE SHARK

The great white shark is the most voracious fish living in the open sea. It is also one of the largest—growing nearly twenty feet in length, and weighing upwards of 2,500 pounds. With rows of two-inch long razor-sharp teeth, it is altogether an efficient instrument of swift and sudden death. The ability of the great white shark to swallow large prey is attested to by the discovery of a whole horse found inside the body of one taken in Australia some years ago. Above we see a luckless scuba diver in the act of being devoured piecemeal by a great white shark.

A GREEK SPONGE DIVER ENCOUNTERS A GIANT MORAY EEL, 1907

A free diver with a net bag around her neck—and carrying a rock to speed her descent to the coral head from which she means to pluck sponges—is shown above in a surprise encounter with a giant moray eel, a vicious predator which will attack anything that moves. The moray eels of the Mediterranean grow to more than ten feet in length and are among the most mysterious creatures of the sea. They are sometimes brilliantly colored: one recently observed in the Caribbean was nearly five feet long, and white with bright purple and lavender streaks and spots all over its body.

In 1973, at Palancar Reef in the Gulf of Mexico, a scuba diver—on poking his fingers into a coral hole—was seized by a moray eel that dragged his hand into the hole. Unable to free his fingers from the teeth of the beast, the diver had to hack off his own hand at the wrist with his diving knife in order to escape with his life, before either the air in his tank ran out or wandering sharks in the vicinity—scenting blood—attacked him.

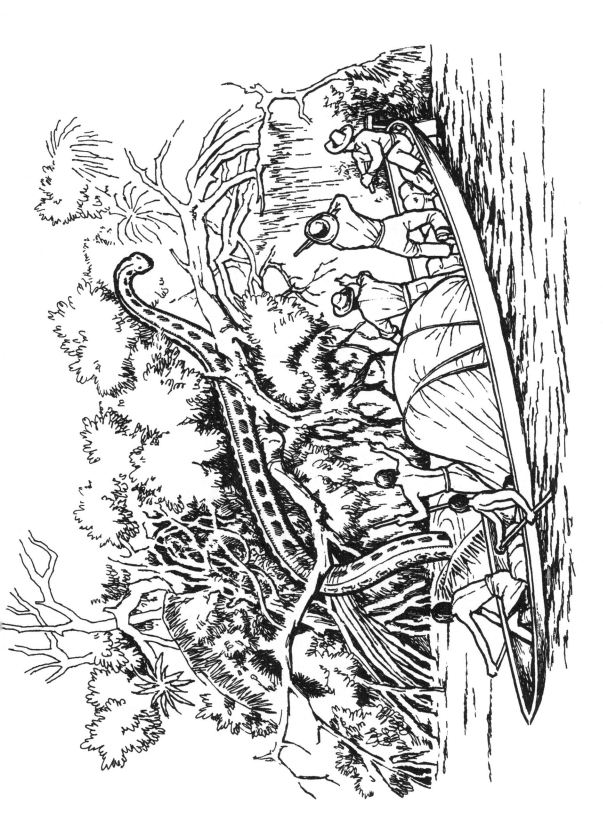

A GIANT ANACONDA OF THE RIO ABUNA, BRAZIL, 1907

In 1907, a British scientific expedition penetrated deep into the vast Amazon forest of Brazil and traversed hitherto unexplored areas of the rain forest in search of giant snakes rumored to live along the Rio Abuna. Major Percy Fawcett, one of the expedition's leaders, shot a sixty-two-foot long anaconda that was encountered along the river bank. Natives of the region claimed that these snakes often attacked boats in the river, and that some anacondas measuring over eighty feet in length had been captured.

THE LEVIATHAN

The Leviathan is a monstrous creature described in the biblical book of Job: "Who can open the doors of his face? His teeth are terrible round about. His scales are his pride . . . Out of his mouth go burning lamps and sparks of fire leap out . . . He maketh the deep to boil like a pot : . . . Upon earth there is not his like, who is made without fear." The Leviathan fits the description of a mythical creature—half fish and half dragon. Shown above is a medieval depiction of this behemoth, accompanied by what appears to be its offspring.

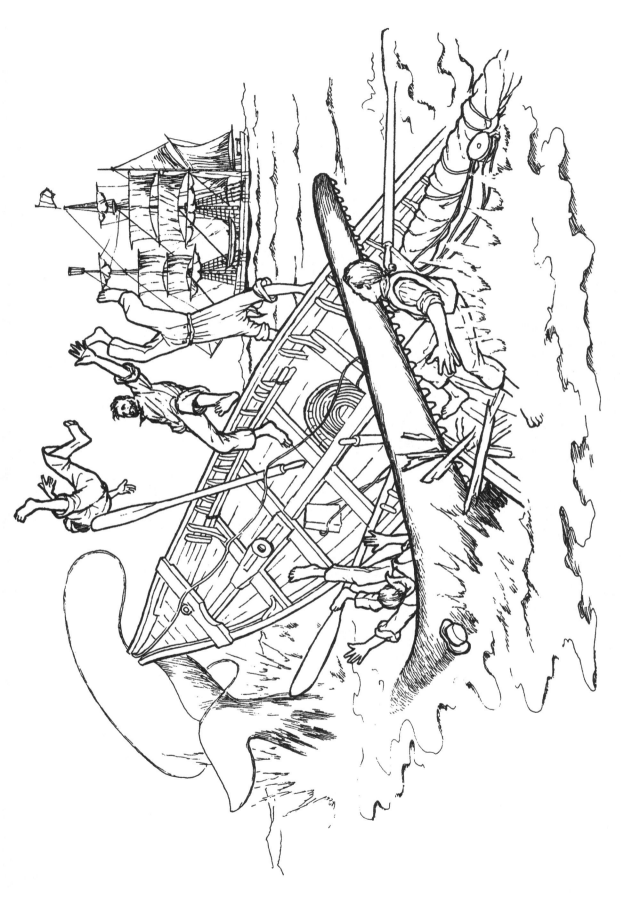

SPERM WHALE ATTACKING A WHALE BOAT, 1820

Shown above is an event commonplace among sailors who hunted whales. The sailor in the foreground is about to be crushed by the lower jaw of the wounded whale as the monster rolls over and lunges at the boat. Whales are the largest living creatures. A female blue whale measuring 110 feet in length was taken in the ocean waters of the Antarctic; she weighed over 190 tons or 380,000 pounds.

THE MONSTER OF PABLO BEACH, FLORIDA, 1891

In 1891, bathers at Pablo Beach, Florida reported seeing—less than a quarter of a mile offshore—a huge snake-like creature rise up straight into the air to a height of perhaps thirty feet: "No tail was visible, the monster twisted around, its head swung from side to side, and then it slid back down into the sea." All the bathers interviewed agreed that the monster was a shiny black color with greenish tints and a whitish belly, with a long forked tongue like that of a snake. The above illustration is based on a drawing that was done from the descriptions given to the local newspaper.